Conversations With

Sasquatch

Book 1
The Encounter

Richard Rensberry

Published by: QuickTurtle Books LLC®

https://www.booksmakebooms.com

ISBN: 978-1-940736-68-6
Published in the United States of America

This book is dedicated to my friend,
Tecumseh.
May his Spirit always live
within the stone without time.

There is a glossary in the back of this book for uncommon and Sasquatch terms

The Encounter

1

I have had to readjust my beliefs and rethink many an opinion since I met a Sasquatch while out hunting for morel mushrooms in Lewiston, Michigan. I had no idea that these mushrooms were high on their list of dietary delicacies. They prize and love them.

I would have been afraid and crapped my pants if it hadn't been for the long outstretched arm that offered me a half eaten morel. There was nothing aggressive or hostile in this gesture. He effused a welcoming aura of curious friendliness.

I took the half-eaten morel and popped it into my mouth. As I shook my head affirmatively, I offered him my paper sack that contained about twenty morels and two or three beefsteaks I had gathered along a cedar ridge beside Big Creek.

It was then that I noticed the pure silence that had fallen over the forest. The crows look-out caws had vanished, the squirrels had shushed their chatter and rattle in the trees. Not even a bluejay or a mosquito was daring a peep.

I struggled to swallow the copper taste that had encroached to dry my mouth.

Sasquatch smiled. He had jaws filled with yellow teeth and eyes that twinkled with delight.

"Thank you," he said, and jiggled his lips like a horse as it eats a sugar cube off your hand.

"You're welcome," I replied with another swallow.

"There's a storm in the air," Sasquatch offered with a gesture towards the sky, "the ozone is lifting my hairs." He proceeded to run his hand a few inches above his upper chest where I could see the hairs stand up as if a magnet were being run over a cache of metal shavings. He abruptly slapped his chest and laughed. It sounded eerily like the shriek of an eagle guarding its kill.

The sky was clear, but I thought I could hear a distant rumble of thunder to the west. I couldn't remember any rain being in the forecast. I had come dressed only in jeans, a polo shirt and sneakers.

"You humans are such frail creatures," he said. "I remember when you were more like us, hunters and gatherers of the health and fruits of The Creator."

I really couldn't tell if he was speaking to me verbally or telepathically. There was such a sense of otherworldliness. I had a hard time getting a grip on my racing thoughts and emotions. In the absence of abject fear, I felt a combination of elation and serenity. I guess it was what you'd call dumbstruck.

"Not much of a talker, are you?" he asked and popped a fresh mushroom into his mouth.

"I have never met a Sasquatch before," I managed.

"Not many a human has," he whispered conspiratorially. "You are the first in many thousands of years I have spoken to. You are the chosen one."

"I am honored," I humbly croaked.

"I am not so sure you should be. You humans are blowing it. You are blind to the world of the Sasquatch. You have lost the memory and instinct of your body's genes and the very essence of your immortal soul."

A darkness crept stealthily over the ridge. Lightning flashed and a huge clap of thunder reverberated off and rattled my teeth. I began to shiver uncontrollably as Sasquatch melted into the rain with a welcoming gesture meant for me to follow him there to wherever there was going to be.

2

Talking to a Sasquatch would probably qualify me as being a delusional schizophrenic or having some such mentally manufactured label from the Diagnostic Manual of Mental Disorders. Rest assured, I am more sane than the writers and creators of that psychiatric flap-trap. As Sasquatch said in our first conversation a little over a week ago, "Humans are blind to the world of the Sasquatch."

Exactly why I was chosen I haven't got a clue. All I know is that today I have an appointment to meet with him once again near that auspicious cedar ridge that runs along the banks of Big Creek, in Lewiston, Michigan.

I do not take this meeting lightly. The fear that was inexplicably absent during our first encounter is in full force as I lock my Mazda and begin my traipse into the greening woods.

As always, I find myself getting unwound and relaxed by the sanctuary of the forest. There is a lush carpet of fresh moss, wintergreen and huckleberry as I begin to cut a trajectory toward the ridge where I had previously shared mushrooms with a being that claimed to be immortal. As I walk, I am suddenly struck with the notion that Sasquatch might like a bag of fresh wintergreen. I, myself, love to chew on the minty leaves, which are cool and relaxing. I kneel down, pluck a new sprout and pop it into my mouth. I then gather a few handfuls of the dark green fingers and slip them into the small Ace Hardware bag I always carry for gathering purposes. I succinctly remember Sasquatch telling me that humans had once been much more attuned to the gathering of the medicinal and nutritional gifts of nature. Is it possible my penchant for such was what had drawn this Bigfoot to engage me?

I don't know. There are doubts. I'm still feeling a bit dumbstruck and unbelieving. I have to work quite hard to suspend my recurring thoughts that Sasquatch was nothing more than a figment of my overactive imagination. Had I eaten (like some have suggested) the wrong mushroom by mistake? Was it possible I had simply hallucinated and manufactured my whole Sasquatch experience from the far reaches of a childhood memory?

Over the years, I must admit, I really hadn't thought much about Sasquatch. I've had no particular reason to do so. I'm a busy person, both purposeful and happy. I think little of the past and focus on the present and the future.

As I continue my trek towards Big Creek, my childhood memory of Sasquatch floods back as if a dam has burst inside my head. I find myself emotionally present in the excitement of the time, the utter bug-eyed blinking and wiping of my eyes during those fateful moments I laid eyes on him bathing in the river near my fishing hole. I am overcome with a hot flash of perspiration. Adrenalin rushes and vibrates through my body as I re-experience running helter-skelter up the bank of the river to reach the deer camp where my father is playing poker and drinking whiskey with his pals.

I breathlessly arrive as Al Kaline is stepping up to the plate with runners on first and third in the top of the ninth in a tight game against the Minnesota Twins. My dad and his pals are glued to the tinny squawk of a small transistor radio, intently listening as Ernie Harwell sets the stage for the next pitch.

I shake my father's arm violently to get his attention and shriek incoherently about the monster bathing in the river. My dad's eyes blink rapidly as he slowly tries to bring me into focus. When he finally registers my presence, he frowns uncompre-hendingly and remains as lethargic as a toad.

"Not now!" he grumbles.

I tug and push even harder, beseeching him to come and see the hairy man that looks bigger than a bear.

"Sorry guys," he groans, "the young tyke is always dreaming up ghosts and things that go bump in the night."

"No!" I exclaim, "He's really there! He's down by the river where the sunfish are!"

"Now son, go play. We'll all be ready to leave in a few. Right now the Tiger's are trying to beat the Twins. Let your dad finish his game."

Forgotten and dismissed, I am overwhelmed by the force of his rejection and disbelief. Coming from my dad, it presses down hard on my young heart. He hadn't even considered for a moment that what I had seen could possibly be true. I was just a kid with nothing better to do than make things up. And yes, I often did make things up, just not Sasquatch taking a bath in the river.

As I neared Big Creek I shook off the memory and began my gradual descent down the ridge toward our destined meeting spot. As I did so, the hackles on my neck suddenly stood straight up and goose flesh prickled down my arms and back. Once again, the woods fell eerily silent. All my senses snapped to the present and I reflexively reached for my absent Beretta which I had purposely left in the car.

3

As a hunter, I know how difficult it can be to move through the forest stealthily. You have to be completely in tune with your body and your surroundings as to not crackle a leaf or snap a twig. It is an art rarely achieved in our modern world. I have a Native American friend named Tecumseh that can do it. He's a real spooky character in that regard. His name means from "one place to another" and he is the epitome of being able to move quickly and silently in any environment.

I have no concept of how Sasquatch could appear like Tecumseh out of thin air. I never heard him. It was like one of Tecumseh's tricks of sneaking up behind me and breathing on my neck. I was certain that if I turned around, he'd be there.

He was.

As before, there was nothing in his demeanor that imparted any kind of aggressiveness. Sasquatch's face looked serene and soft, his eyes twinkled with recognition. All the remaining tension that I had been harboring evaporated.

I instinctively reached out and offered him the bag of wintergreen. He deftly received the sack in his huge right hand, stuck two fingers from his left into the sack and pulled out a single leaf of wintergreen. He crinkled it between his fingers and put it to his nose. He took a deep breath, relished the aroma and let out a guttural sigh that was more like a vibration than a sound.

"Pippsissewa," he chanted. "Pippsissewa."

I tilted my head at the amusing combination of sound and vibration. It was like being tickled.

"The Anishinaabe Indian name for the wintergreen," he tells me, "ancestors of the Chippewa."

"It seems like just yesterday," he adds, "that our kind co-existed with these peoples who enjoined the forest, sky, and waters to their spirit. Did you know that right where you are standing is Anishinaabe sacred ground?"

I reflexively move back a few inches.

Sasquatch lets out a guttural chuckle, flips his hairy arms and hands me a flattish polished stone.

It is surprisingly cool to the touch. I recognize it as lapis lazuli. Its celestial blue signifies gods and power, spirit and vision. It is a universal symbol of wisdom and truth.

"It was found here by a Chippewa medicine man." Sasquatch tells me. "It is said that Big Creek and the Chippewa will eternally run within it."

"Beautiful," I respond, and reach to hand it back.

Sasquatch deliberately sits on his hands, vibrates his lips, rolls his eyes and shakes his head. I immediately understand that he has no intention of taking back the stone. Like the Pippsissewa leaves I had gifted to him, the stone is now a gift to me.

"Thank you," I say, awed by this generous and thoughtful gesture. "I will treasure it as a symbol of ancient wisdom and friendship."

Sasquatch tilts his head and gives me a wry smile. I get the impression he thinks he has achieved some sort of leverage over my emotions with the stone.

"Am I trespassing?" I ask a bit befuddled.

"Some would think so," he says. "Unlike the Anishinaabe, your brethren now believe they are more important and deserving than a toad or the rock it sits on."

"I...," I began, but he shushes me with a forceful exhale.

"Your human spirit is large, like makwa, the bear. The blue stone is in your eyes. The toad does not fear you and will not pee in your hand. The trout and the forest embrace you like a brother. Come back as often as you like. I will know you are near and I will always find you."

I am in wonder of this huge Being, his eloquence of speech and carriage. It is almost as if I can suspend the fact that I am talking to a Sasquatch. "I appreciate that," I say. "I do embrace and respect the forest and plan to come rather often to see you. Does your kind give names to each other, and if so, what is yours?"

"I am known as Loquius. It means teacher with many tongues," he explains.

It is pronounced with three syllables instead of two. It's a name that seems to demand one to listen as the last two syllables tail off succinctly into a quiet hush.

"I am known as Richard," I say. "It means strong or brave leader."

We nod at each other in simultaneous acknowledgement. I inexplicably feel compelled to extend my index finger at the exact same moment Sasquatch extends his. The tips of our fingers touch and any doubts or reservations about Sasquatch being a hallucination or a figment of my imagination are vanquished. He is a fully sentient being of significant intelligence and complex emotions. The deep crevices in his face signify to me an uncharted wisdom and a self-awareness that has spanned the ages. He is truly Loquius.

4

The only person I trust to share my Sasquatch experiences with is Tecumseh. If my mother were still alive, she would be the other, but she passed on an unbelievable twenty years ago.

I meet Tecumseh at his trailer west of Comins. He lives on the edge of a Michigan State Forest he calls Tecumseh's Reservation. For all intents and purposes, it really is his personal playground. No one else hardly ventures there and if they happen by, Tecumseh has ways of scaring the crap out of them and they seldom come back. I have had lots of laughs about his stories of city folk dropping their drawers to take a dump and then hightailing it bare-assed back to the nearest civilization.

The weather is drearily overcast, but humid and warm. I break out into a sweat as we light a fire in the stone pit that will retain a cache of hot coals for a fish fry. I have never seen Tecumseh sweat. It can be a hundred degrees with 100% humidity and he still looks cool and comfortable.

"Caught some real orange beauties," Tecumseh offers, "you should have come with me."

"Sorry, I wanted to talk to you about that," I say, seeing my opening to broaching my recent encounters with Sasquatch. "I was a bit engaged. I've had a couple of conversations with a Bigfoot."

Tecumseh stops what he is doing and gives me that penetrating look only a man of high virtue can give. My eyes don't waver.

He nods, "Chiha Tanka, My Elder Brother. Did Sasquatch have anything significant to say?"

"Yes, he said the human race is blowing it."

Tecumseh laughs mirthlessly. "The same warning I have been poking into your ears since the day we met. Do you believe him?"

"I believe you, don't I?" I counter with a jab.

"My Elder Brother only speaks to deliver important messages about a turn of events or a prophesy of magnitude. What he says should be regarded with utmost respect. He is a special Being. He is translator and mentor into the consciousness that runs through all of life."

"I didn't know you had such inside knowledge." I exclaim. "Have you met this Chiha Tanka, as you call him?"

Tecumseh shakes his head negatively. "That connection is the domain of medicine men. It is for those that guide us between the physical and spiritual worlds. I am a hunter not a healer."

"He is troubled about man and the future," I say. "He has invited me back for further conversations. I am eager and believe he has much more to impart to me, and, in his own words, "to my brethren". I am a good listener as well as an astute and sensitive interrogator."

"You are worthy," Tecumseh replies, "but, be careful."

"What harm could possibly come in talking to him?" I reply.

"If you should wander and get lost between this world and his, I may not be able to bring you back," he says.

I believe I am first witness to seeing sweat on Tecumseh's brow.

He turns abruptly to the task of melting some fat and peanut butter in his cast iron skillet. Fresh caught brook trout fried in peanut butter is a meal worthy of the gods themselves.

5

On my return to Big Creek, I am aware of some recent activity by other humans. It is not only the physical signs, like the matted down grass and discarded cigarette butts, but also the remnants of their auras. People leave in their wake good or bad vibrations that can hang around and be felt from here to eternity unless cleansed from the emotionally disturbed space. What I am feeling at the moment is not good, and it isn't long before I find a half dozen empty beer cans and several Twinkie wrappers scattered about.

I have never known beer and Twinkies to mix well with the forest. I am hoping it is just a sign of some rebellious teenagers getting away from the claustrophobic demands of their parents, and what I am seeing is discarded pieces of their rebellion and carelessness that have been shed like the skin of a snake.

My hopes get permanently dashed when I find more cigarette butts and a game camera locked in place to a small sapling of birch. There is a generous pile of untouched corn a few yards away from the lens that snaps my picture. I stick out my tongue and give it the finger.

Tecumseh would throw a fit if he saw this disrespectful approach to the fine art of hunting. I can literally hear one of his angry rants echoing through the forest as I decide what to do.

"They leave their ugly scent behind like mangy dogs that seem to have a purpose to piss on everything," Tecumseh rails. "They are thankless of all but their own gratification. I weep when I think about how the ancestors of such vile men invaded our tee-pees with their spirits of evil. I pray our eternal wills continue to be reborn without such an abominable weakness for whiskey."

I look around and heft a broken hardwood bow about the size and shape of a baseball bat. I contemplate and weigh it for my purpose. Knowing I have been captured on the camera, I have decided prudence would be my best course of action.

I wind up and take a healthy cut and catch the camera square in the face. It explodes into different pieces and is not easy to gather back together, but I find the photo chip and slip it into my pocket. The rest of the camera pieces and every other sign of human presence, I put in my gathering bag. All that is left is the cable and lock still wrapped around the birch. I apologize in the name of Tecumseh and cut the cable free.

I then backtrack and gather the beer cans and Twinkie wrappers, finger-rake the grasses back to standing the best I can, and collect all the cigarette butts. I am happily gratified to feel the forest rejoice.

With the area cleansed of trash and bad vibrations, I am able to return to contemplating my original purpose. I had been looking forward to another philosophical melding with my Big Foot friend, Loquius.

I have been pondering, that if the Sasquatch are immortal beings that have roamed this planet since the beginning of time, then they have survived the endless disasters of climate change, including ice ages, volcanos, earthquakes, drought, famine, asteroids, and even pandemics.

Man is relatively new to the game, and what is most important in this age of narcissism, are the symbiotic relationships that have and can be further developed between man and nature; each one can enhance the other when common sense and basic ethics are applied to such things as forestry, farming, housing, and industry. Even cities can be redesigned with regenerative energy and agriculture in mind. Man is basically good and will strive for the greatest good for all concerned when he realizes that one lifetime is but a growing and cleansing journey for his immortal soul. To survive, you have to learn that you do not shit in the bed to which you must return.

I hope to garner much more insight into what answers Sasquatch might have to help the human race as it seemingly hurtles unawares towards oblivion.

As I trek, I am elated to have removed the footprints of the litterbugs and their bad vibes. The forest has returned to its harmonious songs within itself. I hear the distant drumming of a partridge, the chatter of squirrels, and the peeping of some snipes at the edge of a meadow filled with dancing grasses. A porcupine scuttles over a log, parks it itself in a defensive posture and raises its quills as I pass nearby.

The walk to meet Sasquatch is over two miles of ever changing terrain. The forest is rife with organic smells and subtle changes of temperature. I have come to recognize many sun dappled openings verdant with ferns as well as groves of various trees. I am traversing the edge of the hardwoods that are easier to navigate than the thick cedars, tag alders and small pines that thrive next to the creek.

It is on the ridge where the hardwoods turn to cedars that Sasquatch appears. I am immediately struck by the aggressiveness portrayed in his muscular stance. There is nothing soft or serene in his posture towards me. My first instinct is to cut and run, but I will myself to keep my poise and hold my ground.

He vocalizes an unearthly bugle of screeching sounds that all but rattle my bones. Instantly, there is movement to his right and another Sasquatch appears at his side.

6

I witness what seems to be a heated discussion with agitated sounds and hand motions before the aggressor reluctantly backs down and withdraws into the trees.

My body is literally vibrating from an overdose of adrenaline racing unchecked through my veins. My heart is pounding hard enough to make my eardrums jump, and I notice I have been probably holding my breath for the duration of the encounter. The combination of excitement and fear has me feeling woozy and wobbly on my feet. I have to kneel to regain my equilibrium, and before I can get back to my feet, I observe the remaining Sasquatch advancing rapidly towards me.

I have no way of defending myself. My stomach is doing flip-flops as I struggle to regain my balance and stand up. I abruptly toss my cookies, advance a couple of steps and fall flat on my face.

I don't ever recall fainting or passing out at any time in my life up until now. I have been knocked unconscious by blunt force, but never by mental or emotional trauma. The heaviness that descends over me isn't a total oblivion without sound or sensation, it is more like watching things unravel from a great distance. It reminds me of looking through the wrong end of a telescope. At the end of the tiny dot of light I see a face, the face of my friend, Loquius.

I know I have been lifted because I am gliding through the forest as if I have wings. There is a blur of green foliage and a strange tart smell like that of fermenting fruit.

I am aware of a drop in temperature a few seconds before I am completely submerged in the ice cold waters of Big Creek. The shock is enough to jolt me upright and make me gulp for breath. As I come fully awake, I am once again hefted into the air where I experience my surroundings from the strange perspective of what it was like when I was a child at the mercy of an adult.

I am whisked through the forest with a confidence and speed I have only experienced on a trusted horse. As a rider, you learn to never fight their inherent certainty of balance and instinct, you always strive to go with the flow and help their gait. So that is what I did. I put my trust in Sasquatch.

7

We travel some distance before Loquius slows his gait and speaks.

"We have crossed over," he tells me. "I have risked a great deal. I could be exiled for breaking a sacred oath not to bring another human to our land. Our last attempt to help your world was not successful."

"Help our world?" I ask, shaken, "In what way?"

"That is a long story," he responds.

We come to a halt in a meadow filled with black-eyed Susan, Indian paint-brush and wild strawberry. As I take in the rich scenery, my senses are accosted by the shear brilliance of the flower colors and the way their auras illuminate the air above the plants. The aroma is exquisitely intoxicating.

Loquius lowers me gingerly to my feet. I become aware for the first time just how tall and broad in girth he is, towering over me by more than a yardstick. His thighs are as big around as my torso. His hair is glistening from grey to a bluish-black in the sunlight, and his skin is a radiant brown that I had not noticed in our previous meetings.

"Welcome to my home," he says with a broad sweep of an arm.

The landscape appears beautifully wild and yet tamed. It does not resemble the Big Creek terrain I am acquainted with in my roaming. Things are all out of kilter. The sky is much too blue and there are gigantic trees I do not recognize. And as I have mentioned, the flowers are much larger and brighter than they should be.

"Where, exactly is this place you call home?" I ask, and run my hand over my head to check for any knots that would signify the possibility of a concussion.

"You have entered Cross Over," he tells me. "This is the alternative path that Earth is traveling under the care of the Sasquatch. It is not the Earth path from which your mechanistic and technological race has evolved."

Sasquatch reaches down and scoops up a handful of organic matter and soil. It is literally pulsing in his hand and through his fingers with a myriad of living organisms. There are worms, grubs and an abundance of small wigglers I have never seen.   It smells pungently organic and fresh. It is black, moist, and rich as my sister's chocolate cake.

"This is your planet in Cross Over," he states. "You will not be able to stay. There are those in the Council that feel man is undeserving of Sasquatch help. They want nothing to do with your rapid descent away from natural law and your selfish ascent into narcissism. They believe you are committing suicide."

I am caught off guard and offer no defense to these blunt charges coming from a Sasquatch.

"Some members of the Council do not think that your demise will effect our demise," Loquius continues, "but I believe differently. I have supplied to the council, indisputable evidences of the technological poisons that have been seeping through at the Cross Over edges. There is evidence that shows that man-made poisons are rapidly eroding and shrinking not only your world but ours. Your human selfishness, pesticides, herbicides, 5G microwaves, pharmacopeia and genetic engineering are rapidly destroying your world and will destroy ours along with it."

I decidedly want to wake up and get back to a place called Sanity. This is nuts! I am being lectured by a Sasquatch.

"Do you recognize the name Ted Kaczynski?" Loquius asks.

Somewhere in my brain the name rings a bell, but I cannot put a finger on it. "Sounds familiar," I say, shrug my shoulders and relinquish to not remembering.

"In your world he is known as the Unabomber. In our world he is known as "The Man Who Crossed Over". He unexpectedly came to our world without any help from our kind. How he found his way, we can only guess. Subsequently he was invited back many succeeding times by the Council and acquired much knowledge that was to be translated for the benefit of mankind. It was our goal to help reverse the downward spiral in which your race is caught. We were hopeful. Unfortunately, he lost his way as well as his sanity. His frustrations led to a warped attempt through force to get your world's attention. It continued to escalate when the wisdom he had to offer was continually ignored and ridiculed."

My memory is finally jogged and it all comes back to me. Ted Kaczynski was an ex-Harvard professor arrested by the FBI after his anti-technological manifesto was published by major newspapers. He had disintegrated into a domestic terrorist and a murderer targeting business executives with sophisticated letter bombs. I remember a picture of a disheveled character being led away in handcuffs from a mountain cabin in Colorado.

"Mankind rejected the knowledge and warnings we helped him author as the ramblings of a psychopath," Loquius imparts, spinning his finger at his temple in one of our symbolic gestures for craziness.

I would find what I am hearing to be too incredulous to believe if it weren't coming from a Sasquatch in a place called Cross Over. I find myself seeking solace by rubbing my recently acquired lapis lazuli stone between thumb and forefinger. It is a habit I have fallen into at odd times. I am now coming to some understanding of the meaning of Loquius' wry smile when I had taken the stone as a gift. In some way, I had already crossed over.

I haven't a clue about what Ted Kaczynski had tried to communicate besides an anger potent enough to maim and kill people with his sophisticated packages.

"You can't stay long," Loquius says, "but I want you to meet my family."

8

We enter a grove of giant shade trees at the edge of the meadow. The leaf shape on these unusual trees is that of an oak and I can see clusters of small acorns in their formative stages. The trees themselves have long interwoven branches of which some of them touch the ground and then bend skyward once again. It is hard to distinguish bouncing limbs from trunks. Underfoot is a lush carpet of moss and ground cover very similar to what I am accustomed to on my treks along Big Creek.

Within the grove is a circular clearing where a substantial mound twice my height dominates the opening. It is covered in flowering shrubs in various stages of bloom. Loquius uses his arm to brush aside a tangled mass of branches and exposes a woven and braided grass doorway that leads into the mound. I am ushered into a room filled with soft light, filtered through portholes that appear to be extremely large translucent fish scales. There are hanging log and pottery containers rife with herbs, cucumbers, tomatoes and melons. The atmosphere is humid, warm and totally welcoming to my human senses.

I am led down a stone hallway deeper into the mound where a miniature Sasquatch dashes out and leaps into Loquius' arms. The verbal exchange is indecipherable, but physically I see much intimacy and warmth. Loquius sets her back on the ground at his knees.

"This is Pureesis, she is my youngest," Loquius beams, "her name means "pure of heart". My mate and eldest are in the weaving room making seeding mats."

I smile at the shy youngster as she clings to Loquius' huge leg.

The weaving room is draped with fibers hanging from pole frames. The strands are multi-colored in an assortment of lengths and widths. At a wooden table, stand his mate and eldest lifting and shuffling wooden slats in a rapid-fire slap-dance. They are totally engrossed in their work and remain unaware of our presence until Loquiis makes a clicking sound with his tongue and teeth. Both look up and lose control of their precise rhythm when they see me standing next to Loquius.

I notice that his eldest is a young Sasquatch, tall, but not nearly as heavyset as Loquius, himself. His mate is much shorter with pronounced breasts and a smaller head.

Loquius says something I cannot understand, pointing me out with his hand. A small discussion ensues and then they indicate an acceptance with a nod and a smile.

"Glad to meet you," I say cordially.

"My eldest, Leeitus. And Loquiili, my mate."

Loquiili gestures towards me and speaks, again an incomprehensible language that eerily sounds electronic.

"She wants to know if you would like some tea and something to eat?" Loquius asks.

The mention of food makes me realize that I am starving as well as parched. Not knowing what to expect, I respond, "Please."

Leeitus fetches a wooden cup and Loquiili pours me an amber colored liquid from a sun heated bamboo tube. The tea is earthy, sweet and tangy.

"Delightful," I tell her with a smile.

Loquiili looks pleased and gestures me into a dining area to sit at a bench positioned before a hanging table. Pureesis lets go of her daddy's leg and ventures over to sit on the bench near me. Her big eyes filled with a shy curiosity.

A huge platter of vegetables is carried in by Leeitus and placed in front of us. There are thick slabs of tomatoes dressed with herbs, cucumbers and radishes sliced diagonally, covered with what look like flower petals and green peas still in their pods. All are deeply colored and vibrantly fresh.

Loquiili gestures towards the plate and rubs her belly. I take this as a green light invitation to eat and gingerly pick up a tomato slab. When I take a bite, the taste is robust and delicious. I devour it in four more bites.

Again, Loquiili looks pleased.

I sample a radish which is pungent and mildly hot. The cucumbers are crisp, cool and juicy. Most of all, I am enamored by the peas, they are tender and bursting with a musky, deep, sweet flavor. I cannot withhold myself and eat them all as my body craves for their nourishment and rejoices in the fulfillment.

Soon, everyone is nodding and smiling. My tea cup is replenished and Loquius joins me with a generous helping of tomato slabs. Pureesis edges nearer to me and reaches out with a finger to touch my flannel shirt. We both recoil, then smile, before she once again extends her timid hand. I oblige by offering my arm and fingers for her exploration.

"As I said," Loquius interjects, "You will not be allowed to stay beyond a quick perusal of our border. We must cross back over, shortly."

"There are no other humans here," I query.

"None that I know of," Loquius says quietly. "You are not supposed to be here."

I nod. Coming to grips with the idea that I have entered an alternate Earth universe where no humans are allowed is not a comfortable nor everyday occurrence.

9

"It is crepuscule hour, our sacred time of positive prayer and no one will be out and about at this time," Loquius states. "It is now that I can and would like to give you a glimpse of Cross Over, the land that lies between our two diverse worlds."

He leads me out into the dusky half-light through a different egress from his many chambered home. Leeitus has joined us and we walk along a mossy path back into the trees and follow a stream that is most likely Big Creek as it has evolved over time between our worlds. We emerge into an orchard of fruit trees, grapes, berries and plots of other crops turning to purple-black in the diminishing light.

Loquius reaches out and picks a multi-fingered leaf off a waist high plant. When he shows it to me, I think I recognize it as hemp or marijuana.

"Kenaf," he says with reverence, "millions of years old. It is the best for creating most everything of use in our culture. Leeitus and Loquiili were weaving its fibers into seed mats when we arrived."

"Kenaf?" I ask. "I believe in our world it is called marijuana."

"No, it is not Nawak'osis, The Dreamer. Unlike humans we do not need or want such substances to alter our thoughts or emotions. We embrace all thoughts and emotions as proper and good as long as they are appropriate to the circumstance. Nawak'osis is lazy and irresponsible, he does not allow a farmer or warrior to do what is necessary if and when it is necessary."

I recall marijuana's addictive indulgences and remember it did make me lazy and irresponsible when I was a young man. It had been a juvenile trap that I had had to learn to grow up and out of.

"I understand," I respond.

"The kenaf plant has the same properties as nawak'osis minus the temptations. It does not contain any mind altering properties, only nutritional and artisan properties that enhance the quality of our lives."

Loquius pops the kenaf leaf into his mouth, picks another and hands it to me with a gesture to give it a try.

I nibble on one of its fingers. It is unlike anything I have ever tasted, very earthy, spicy and tender.

"Very good," I say.

"Not only is it edible, it has thousands of other uses from cleansing and invigorating the soil, to feeding and healing life itself. It is in your world but mostly ignored."

I am unfamiliar with ever hearing about such a plant. Even industrial hemp contains measurable amounts of the drug THC that induces the euphoric high so sought after by millions of humans across our world.

Darkness is descending quickly and Loquius and Leeitus are beginning to blend into the background. Their hides are becoming completely lost in the dark silhouettes of trees and all I am able to discern are their slightly lighter faces and gesturing hands.

"We must go," Loquius states. "I will help you cross over near your machine so you do not have to flounder about in the woods of your dark world."

Once again I am scooped up into his strong arms and speedily whisked off and back into the forest. I am overcome with a feeling of child-like helplessness.

10

I type Ted Kaczynski into the Google search bar and find myself reading what is known as the Unabomber Manifesto.

Even without my recent insight into its origins, I am transfixed by the amount of observational reality that is contained in the man's analysis of our troubled race. At the same time, I am deeply perplexed and troubled as to how this apparent wisdom was perverted into the violence and force that the Unabomber chose to use in his attempt to halt the perpetrators of science and technology. Was he that frustrated and angry with his fellow man as to not pursue and garner intellectual agreement from like-minded colleagues? Did his mind get stretched beyond its rational capacity, unable to accept the fact that he once was deeply entwined in that technological system he despised? Did he struggle with the fact that he was human and not Sasquatch? In his arrest photograph I can certainly see a resemblance to the young Leeitus, both in the Unabomber's eyes and his disheveled Sasquatch-like appearance.

My mind is spinning with all these questions and many more. Who was the angry Sasquatch that screamed at me before Loquius had intervened? Am I some kind of replacement for an imprisoned Ted Kaczynski? Had I been rescued or tricked by a cunning Sasquatch by the name of Loquius?

On top of all the questions, I find myself reeling and feeling guilty for being sucked into a manifesto written by a so called domestic terrorist. On the other hand, I have always taken pride in having an open mind and knowing that labels can be deceptive, even to the point of determining who is crazy, the patient or the psychiatrist. I have never believed the FBI nor the press, they have agendas dictated by politics, special interests, and money. Truth unfortunately, has nothing to do with any of those things.

Learning to trust my intuition has been a long and arduous life lesson and my gut feeling tells me Loquius is being straightforward and can be trusted, with both man's and my best interests in mind. If the Unabomber was a failed conduit for the Sasquatch knowledge and help humans need, then so be it, the truth is still the truth no matter who the messenger. I am destined to proceed.

This morning's news is also alarming as I find myself amidst a scene from a science fiction script. The governor of our great state has declared a shut down of all "non-essential" commerce and travel due to a health threat. All citizens are to shelter in place, in essence meaning we have been placed under house arrest to one degree or another. This is not Marshall Law, mind you, this is "for our own good". And I was thinking Ted Kaczynski was nuts.

Seriously, I am peeved. I live in the United States of America, supposedly protected by its Constitution and Bill of Rights, and the governor pretends she has the power to usurp those rights? I would understand and abide by (the best I can) a polite request for common sense, but this egocentric demand for subservient obedience is tyrannical. We're not even supposed to go fishing? Get a grip lady! If I encounter another human being in the forest or on a lake, I make it a point to stay a lot more than six feet away. I am adding the writing of a letter to the Attorney General onto my to do list.

So, (deep breath) with that causative decision, I can get back to the matters at hand. Cross Over, how do I get myself back there?

I am sitting on the ridge overlooking Big Creek where I first encountered Loquius. I have been sitting here for over two hours. The forest is impatient with chattering squirrels, squawking blue jays and an assortment of other dismayed creatures, alarmed not by Sasquatch, but by my human presence. In all that time, I have not seen hide nor hair of Loquius, nor for that matter, any sign at all of his Bigfoot kind. Their aura of existence has vanished. I am left with ruminating on my insecurities of how my life has changed so drastically in the span of the last few weeks and hours. The feeling of loss that is creeping over me is claustrophobic and smothering, as if I am on the verge of a panic attack. I haven't felt this miserable since my stay at college when I found my best friend in bed with my fiancé. I am feeling the inklings of that raw, stimulated anger I had felt back then, piling up behind the dam of my sadness. I remember how the deceit and betrayal by my best friend was one hundred times worse than the unfaithfulness of the girl he seduced. Her, I could forgive, him I could not. There is no rational reason for these broken hearted memories except they are in the same pot being stirred up by the betrayal of trust I am now experiencing through the absence of Loquius.

What if this is as far as it goes? Could I endure the weight of my Cross Over experience if I were never to see Loquius and his family ever again? Will I grow crazy as Ted Kaczynski, sitting on this ridge alone in a forest where Cross Over exists unknown to any other humans but myself and that one locked away in a super-max prison in Colorado?

13

If perchance Tecumseh and I have the Corona virus, a fishing trip will unequivocally ensure no one else will get it. In the case we don't have the virus, a fishing trip will eliminate any possibility of someone that does have it, from infecting us. That's simple common sense and the feeling I get in defying the Governor's ridiculous no fishing order is truly therapeutic in that it has succeeded in lifting me out of the funk of having been stood-up by my Sasquatch friend, Loquius.

Tecumseh and I are unloading my boat and gear to go out trolling for northern pike on a small lake near McKinley.

"You ever been in jail?" I ask Tecumseh.

"You cannot imprison an Indian," Tecumseh replies. "Our spirits are like eagles and the sky and the forest cannot be barred."

"Well, I'm afraid that could get tested if we get caught," I tell him. "The Governor has ordered the DNR to impose fines and imprisonment on anyone that goes on the water with a motorboat."

Tecumseh chuckles and waves his hand in dismissal.

The lake is smooth as glass with a low-hanging mist as we push-off in our twelve-foot aluminum boat with its small Johnson motor.

"Peace lives in the hearts of those with patience," Tecumseh offers as he looks into my tackle box for a lure.

I know he is waiting patiently for a sign from the fishing gods.

The eerie call of a loon rises in solitary mourning from the mist. Tecumseh tilts his head and smiles. He extracts a smallish green and gold daredevil from the box and mouths a little private incantation of thanks. He kisses the lure and settles in his seat, ready and content.

I navigate up the shore to where I have caught many pike on previous trips to the lake. I want to anchor near a drop-off and just cast to see if we can hook into a fish or two.

"What has My Bigfoot Brother, Chiha Tanka, divulged to you, my friend?" Tecumseh broaches as I ease the boat to the edge of the drop-off and lower the anchor.

I realize that so much has transpired since my last conversation with Tecumseh that I wouldn't know even where to begin. Confronted with the act of trying to explain my experiences with Sasquatch and Cross Over has me tongue tied.

Tecumseh gives me his patented penetrating stare until I pull the lapis stone out of my pocket and hand it to him. "He gave me this," I explain, "it is from an ancestor of yours. It is said that Big Creek and the Chippewa will eternally run within it."

Tecumseh closes his eyes and caresses the stone. I have seen him do this kind of thing before. It was Tecumseh from whom I had learned the art of cleaning spaces. It is almost as if he is able to become the things he touches or feels, and by doing so, alter his and their being.

"Yes, my ancestors are here, it is the stone without time," he says as he palms it and taps it to his heart. "You, my friend," he states emphatically, "have the gift of the Mida."

He affectionately returns the stone to my hand

and closes my fingers around it.

"It is filled with the guiding spirits of water. It is said amongst the elders that if you follow the water, you will never get lost."

"But, that is exactly how I feel at the moment, lost," I admit.

"Then you must follow the water. It will show you the way."

I finger the stone and inexplicably get a clear image of Big Creek. Rather than the ridge on which I had sat in wait, I get the image of a bend in the stream where the water rushes and turns black beneath an undercut bank.

"I think maybe I can do that," I say.

Tecumseh's attention is suddenly diverted to his fishing rod and he flicks his wrist. His pole doubles over and jerks rapidly as line screams from his reel.

"Giigoonh na," he proclaims, "too big."

I excitedly grab the net and position myself at the ready, but the big fish is only retrieved a few turns before it turns its mighty head and rolls out of reach. The rod jerks one more time then goes slack as the line pops with a resounding snap. Tecumseh laughs and slaps his thigh in delight.

"Patience, my friend," he says, speaking to the fish. "Our destinies are now forever entwined."

14

I have memorized the voices and idiosyncrasies of more streams than one would think possible during my excursions into the wilds as a trout fisherman. I recall the anointed spot in my vision where the rushing water has carved the black hole beneath the bank of Big Creek. That is a spot where I have fished for brown and brook trout many times in the past.

I am excited and confident that the lapis stone gave me that location as a sign. How these things work is a little beyond my grasp, but I have seen so many instances of this kind of sorcery from Tecumseh that I have no reason to disbelieve the inherent powers of our sixth and higher senses.

Before heading out, I decide to consult my phone to check the Internet for any available data on the strange plant, kenaf, I had been shown and tasted while in Cross Over. Getting a reality on what it is and its properties may prove to be a valuable asset should I be invited back.

I find out it is actually of a species common to our vocabulary. It is a variety of hibiscus, and is common in many parts of the world, especially Asia and Africa. This particular variety, called kenaf, does in some ways resemble marijuana, in both leaf structure and fiber content. It apparently has thousands of beneficial and potential uses, less the liability of teenagers and irresponsible adults running off with it and a pipe to smoke it in.

In packing my essentials, I am once again torn about whether or not to take my gun. I have had a license to carry for many years and have gotten accustomed to its presence at the small of my back while trekking in the wilds. I feel a bit naked without it when there are unexpected dangers that could arise, such as cougars, Massasauga rattlesnakes, and even possibly an angry Sasquatch. But, after deliberating, I finally decide to leave the gun and my phone in the car as I have done on my previous trips to meet Loquius.

Today the woods is damp and lush from a recent rain. Northwood lilies and lady slippers abound in the hardwoods before I drop into the ravine that cradles the creek. Here there are pussy willows and fiddleheads galore. The poplar and birches are in bud and the forest is a symphony of brilliant greens and soft whites. My heart is overjoyed.

Traversing the constant windings of the creek adds a considerable distance to the walk, but today I am enjoying the idea of following the water. It is true that the water always knows where it is going. If you trust it (as in Tecumseh's words) you will never get lost.

Listening to the stream's laughter as it falls over logs and swirls around boulders is a sound that reminds me of children at play in a schoolyard, both are pure of heart and playfully free. It makes me feel the same way in their presence.

A twig pops beneath my right foot and a partridge erupts from a thicket near the rapids that harbored my vision. As I pause in the partridge's wake, the only sound I hear is that of my own breathing and the pounding of my heart on the drums of my ears. It's as if I have entered some sort of vacuum. I feel a tug on the hairs of my arms and neck. Even the rushing rapids seems to shush itself in an attempt to momentarily listen.

The heavy silence is broken by a solitary crow sounding a warning somewhere off in the distance.

Loquius is near, of that I have certainty.

I am filled with both excitement and trepidation, expecting the Sasquatch to appear from the trees at any moment. I am aware of that strange tart smell that is like fermenting fruit. It was prevalent while Loquius whisked me through the forest, in and out of Cross Over.

As I approach the bank of the creek where the water turns black, a recollection of being stalked passes over me. I remember I'd even gone so far as pulling my gun while fishing this exact spot in the past.   Something had been afoot back then, something that had spooked me enough to pull my weapon. I recall racking it up to a curious bear or maybe a cougar keeping an eye on me.

As I stare down into the water, all my nerve endings are tingling. I can feel the spilling water's rush hammering away at the web of tree roots and moss on which I am standing. The sound is constant and relentless as an angry nest of bees. Again, that strange feeling of being stalked.

I have no recollection of how I ended up in the water.

Did I jump or was I pushed?

I struggle, trying to abort panic mode. I am trapped beneath the bank in a tangle of roots. They act like prison bars as the stream's current grabs me and thrusts me deeper into the darkened undercut. I have no choice but to twist and roll with the force of the strong current and pray I come out an opening at the other end. I am knocked about like a fighter against the ropes. My lungs are about to burst when I thankfully stretch my arms for the brilliant sun and suck in a welcome gulp of fresh air.

I am standing waste deep in a pool at the end of the rapids.   My surroundings have no resemblance to the Big Creek wilds I have left on the other side of the undercut bank. Once again I am struck by an array of strong colors emanating from a more tamed and strange landscape. It looks more like a layered garden than a ramshackle forest, and is alive with a cacophony of scurrying animals and rustling birds. The plants themselves look as if they are sentient and rejoicing in each others company, wrapping into each other and hugging like lovers, yet none overwhelming the other. It's a world that looks healthy, happy and vibrantly alive.

My spirits are buoyed as I stumble from the water and sit momentarily on the bank. It is covered with a dense carpet of day-glow green moss. Its texture is soft and cool to the touch.

Pulling off my boots, I wring out my socks. I am a little bruised physically and mentally, but intact, as I struggle to remove my remaining clothes and expose my skin to the moss and warmth of the sun.

In the process of wringing out my pants, I am already calculating and making plans to follow the water south in an effort to cross locate the meadow with the giant oak-like trees I saw on my last visit. I figure I entered the creek about a half mile north of the ridge where Loquius and I last meet. If this is the case, I shouldn't have any difficulty finding and recognizing the brilliant meadow filled with Black-eyed Susans and Indian paintbrush near where Loquius and his family make their home.

I am ready to hide at the drop of my drawers, though I feel no imminent danger. I am sensing along with the other Cross Over lifeforms that there are no Sasquatch about. We are alone.

I look back into the water at my naked reflection. I cannot help but think of Ted Kaczynski. Is this how it all began? Did he too fall into the water and Cross Over so to speak?

16

I am definitely no longer in Lewiston. I see squirrels the size of raccoons and blue jays that could probably pick them up and haul them away. I just stepped over a milk snake that I mistook for a log. It was big enough to swallow both the squirrel and the blue jay together, but thankfully, it forked its tongue and ignored me before slithering on to wherever a Cross Over milk snake might slither.

It is easy going, juking from tree to tree in the park-like forest, nothing like battling the dead falls and thick brush I am accustomed to circumnavigating the woods back home. To my advantage, I am also able to move silently on the soft moss near the creek. I feel the water is not only my guide, but my protector. If I should encounter an unknown Sasquatch, I plan to slip into the water to conceal myself. Not only will the water disguise my body, but also my scent.

As I move stealthily amongst the cover of trees, it is the fermenting smell of a nearby Sasquatch that once again alerts me. Though I cannot see one, I can certainly smell him. I am also aware of the complete silence that always seems to accompany their presence. I freeze, mid-step in the open between trees and try to discern any movements in the periphery of my vision.

Detecting nothing, I crouch in my wrestler's stance and back slowly towards the creek. I almost chuckle at the absurd image that comes to mind. Little old me wrestling a Sasquatch! I choke off the laughter, nestle behind a tree and wait.

A Sasquatch abruptly appears and walks towards me. As I surreptitiously back towards the water, he speaks. I recognize the voice as that of Leeitus.

"You can come out," he says, "my father has been expecting you."

I breathe a sigh of relief and show myself.

"Please, come with me," he says in a friendly manner. His English is clipped and heavily accented, but clear enough to be quite discernible.

I step forward and follow the young Sasquatch as he angles away from the creek, but in the general direction I had already been heading. The forest around us remains relatively free of any debris and quite tame. Leeitus is relaxed, silent and what I perceive to be protective. He slows or stops even if I pause or lag a single step.

After a few minutes we break out of the woods and gently descend into the meadow of which I had become familiar with on my previous visit into Cross Over. It is as beautiful as ever and busy with huge bees laden with pollen. Their unwieldy bodies stagger like drunks after an all day stint at the pub, yet they somehow manage to get airborne from the flowers and bumble off.

Loquius is standing at the row of trees that guard his home. Pureesis is playing at his side and smiles as Leeitus and I approach.

"Richard," Loquius enunciates, "you have listened to the stone. I am sorry you could have been hurt or even killed. My praises go out to you."

"It never crossed my mind," I say, "I was too busy scrapping and clawing. What crossed my mind was that maybe I had been pushed."

"Yes, you are most worthy of the stone and the future that will come with it," he states proudly, as if congratulating himself for my safe arrival.

"And what might this future you speak of have in store?" I ask.

Loquius turns his palms to the landscape and slowly rotates his body in a circle that takes in all of

Cross Over. He smiles. "A gift to man," he proclaims.

17

"You now have the knowledge and ability to travel between our worlds," Loquius tells me as Leeitus brings me a steaming cup of hot tea. It is different from the tea of my previous trip, more flowery and light instead of earthy.

"How will I get back to my world without your help?" I ask. "The current in Big Creek is much too strong to navigate upstream."

"Trust in the stone," he answers, "but not today. For now, you can stay. It is safe here. When the time comes, I will let you know."

As before, I am served a platter of fresh food. It contains an assortment of wooden bowls filled with slightly fermented fruits. There are peaches and apricots as well as berries. They are bursting with flavors that are phenomenal compared to the tasteless fruits I am used to getting from our local groceries in Mio or Lewiston. Accompanying the fruit bowls are crisp slices of some kind of white root. It reminds me of parsnips and together with the fruits, are eaten like chips and dip.

The whole family has joined us. Little Pureesis once again sits by my side. She is infatuated with touching me lightly with her fingers and then giggling. Out of curiosity, I play the game and touch her back. Her fur, though it looks somewhat soft, is quite coarse like the beard of a goat.

"Pureesis," Loquius chastises, "let our guest eat."

The little one whines something in their strange language and appears to pout. Loquiili gets to her feet and comes over and sits next to the little girl. She says something to Loquius in the same strange tongue.

"She wants to help Pureesis get over her infatuation with you. In order to do so, she would like to have Pureesis touch you several times upon her command. Is this okay?" Loquius asks.

"Sure," I respond.

Loquius nods to Loquilli.

She says something to Pureesis and points to my arm. Pureesis touches it and giggles. Loquilli points to my hand. Again, Pureesis touches my hand and giggles.

This procedure of point and touch goes on for several minutes. Pureesis touches various of my body parts until she cheerfully babbles something to Loquilli. They both laugh. Then the procedure is done a few more times without any hesitancy nor giggles on the part of the little girl. She appears relaxed and satisfied with my presence. She and her mother then go about the task of clearing the table as if nothing untoward had happened whatsoever.

"Thank you," Loquius tells me. "Please, finish your tea and fruits."

18

I have the feeling that I am going to be spending the night in Cross Over. The sun has settled behind the trees and long shadows have dappled the bench on which I sit with Loquius. The air is pleasantly warm and moist. It is now Crepuscule Hour and Loquius has informed me that this is the time to cleanse the mind and soul of all things troubling or negative.

"You meditate?" I ask.

"No," he says. "It is what your fellow traveler Ted called visualization. It is more like your world's prayers. It is creating vivid images in one's mind, like a painter of what one wants tomorrow to bring."

"Day dreaming," I proclaim.

"Yes and no," Loquius states, "Please, give it a try. What do you see in your tomorrow?"

"I see you," I say, "and flowers."

"Very good," he replies, "Now, you create what you see. Don't look at what you think tomorrow will be. Put something there to look at. Cause tomorrow, make it real. That is what visualization is. That is creating your tomorrow."

"I have no clue what tomorrow might bring."

"Then you are at the mercy of the wind. You are but a leaf disconnected from the tree. You have no roots into that which gave you life." Loquius states.

"I guess I am more of wanderer," I say, "I like wandering."

"Wandering is fun, but it gets you nowhere unless that is where you intend to go. It is important that you learn how to create reality every day. You are either the cause of tomorrow or the effect of it. That is the problem with your world. It is run by mechanistic attitudes and automaticity. Everyone is content to receive what tomorrow brings them, instead of creating it before it happens. Then you complain about it, argue about it, and even go to war with each other because you blame someone else for the reality you are failing to create."

Taken by his clarity, I ask, "You want me to plan?"

"I want you to cleanse your mind and soul of the past and focus on tomorrow. Fill it with images like the one you saw in the stone. Together, we created the picture of the creek and it brought you here. That is visualization. That is what we do at Crepuscule Hour. Now shush and let me create a better tomorrow."

Telepathy, I am thinking. In order for me to receive the image in Loquius' mind, I had to have been a partner in its creation. I had wanted to come back to Cross Over and with Loquius' help, I had visualized the creek as the way to get here, and here I am.

My curiosity and inkling of understanding has me locked into the game. I try to rid my mind of thoughts and put an image of creation there to look at, instead of worry and think, think. It sounds simple, but it is very difficult to create new pictures distinct from memories already there in my head. After awhile, I am creating and looking at a picture of the Sasquatch that screamed at me just prior to my first visit to Cross Over. I'd like to know why he was there. Why was he screaming at me? I work very hard at creating pictures of him and others here in Cross Over. I finally feel content with my achievement when I open my eyes.

Night has fallen. The sky is a brilliant kaleidoscope of stars swirling with galaxies that makes me dizzy just to look up. They appear so near, I feel I could reach out and touch their vibrancy.

"As you can see, in our world, there is no pollution, so you can touch the stars, you can walk on the moon," Loquius says in reverence, "that's an image of tomorrow worth creating."

19

I am led inside where the table is set for dining. Once again it is an assortment of fruits, flower petals, and vegetables. I see no evidence that the Sasquatch are meat eaters until a huge platter of dried fish is set center table by Leeitus. It looks similar to the smoked lake trout my parents used to relish when I was a kid. They called these large trout, Butter Balls, because of the oily fat that made them so conducive to smoking.

Loquiili follows Leeitus into the room and sets an arrangement of purple lilacs next to the fish.   Both Sasquatches retreat and return with trays filled with tiny wooden cups filled with aromatic spices . One tray is set near to the head of the table, then the others are set at each place setting.

I take some time to inspect my surroundings in the dim light. Though I had been here before, I had been too dumbfounded to pay much attention to the details. I notice there is artificial light of some kind, though it is not very bright. It comes from small portholes in the ceiling and near the floor. The floor is slabs of rock, the ceiling and walls look to be rubbed plaster.

Loquiili calls the family to gather. I am ushered to a chair opposite Loquius at the table. Leeitus and Pureesis sit together to my left and Loquiili sits to my right. It all seems quite formal. Loquius announces something in their tongue I do not understand. It appears to be a prayer addressed in reverence to the food and the heavens.

Upon completion of the prayer, Leeitus stands and serves the food. He first offers a platter to Loquius who points and receives portions of each entree until he nods fulfillment. I am served next. I follow the procedure of pointing and nodding until I am satisfied with the portions. When everyone is served, Loquius once again offers a small prayer in their electronic language.

I watch as they take whatever vegetable or fruit desired and sprinkle it with one of the spices from the small cups.   Once satisfied, they pop them into their mouths. Mimicking Pureesis, I take a peach wedge and sprinkle it with a yellowish powder and chuck it into my mouth. I recognize the spice as a burst of ginger and cinnamon. It is hot and zingy.

The fish has been brined and sun dried to a crisp coating that is lemony tart and peppery. The meal is enjoyed in relative silence, except for the occasional exclamation to compliment each other on the goodness of a specific combination of vegetable, fruit and spice. I find it all delicious and shake my head and smile broadly.

When we are finished, Leeitus clears the table except for the aromatic lilacs near the center. He then returns with a colorfully painted ewer and puts fresh cups before each of us. What is dispensed from the ewer is a deep reddish liquid that has the familiar smell of spirits. To my shock, even Pureesis gets a tiny portion.

Another invocation is spoken and everyone sips their drink.

The heavy liquid reminds me of a rich plum wine served by my brother's Japanese wife, though considerably stronger and more powerful in its rush through my veins.

"A small gift from the land of spirits," Loquius offers.

"I thought your kind did not indulge in such mind altering substances," I say a bit dismayed.

Loquius smiles. "Just one thimble with a nod from the gods, anymore and it takes the day's pleasures away. Anymore and we are reduced to creating a world the likes of yours."

It is the Cross Over sun peeking over the horizon and bleeding a soft glow over my face that awakens me.

My sleep was deep and dreamless, ensconced like a child in a bed of kenaf fluff that had been sewn inside a soft covering made from the plant's woven fibers. It is all quite domestic and homey.

I look around in the half-light in desperate need to relieve myself. Unfortunately, I have not seen nor been indoctrinated on the protocols of doing my duty in a Sasquatch house. Do they just go outside like I do when out in the woods, or do they have some sort of a bathroom?

I cannot endure to wait any longer, so I decide to head for the bushes. In the hallway outside my room I encounter Leeitus standing at the ready. He is perched with his arms crossed near a doorway draped with colorful braided fibers. He rotates and parts the drapery with a nodding gesture for me to enter.

To my relief, the little room contains a huge commode.

Upon inspection, I can see the bowl is waterless and contains what looks like coarse sawdust. There is even a nearby tube of fluff I am certain is to be used as toilet paper. Beside the commode is a scoop and a bucket with the sawdust material. It smells of sage, rosemary and other aromatic herbs. Curious, I reach into the bucket and grab a handful. It is soft and resilient with a spongey texture that reminds me of cigarette filters.

Outside the bathroom, I once again encounter Leeitus.

"We have no time to dawdle," he informs me in his rough clipped voice.

I am urgently lead out the back side of the mound where the mossy path takes us into the trees and along the stream. It is a pleasant morning, cool and redolent with the sweet aromas of a dew dampened dawn in the Cross Over forest. The sky is a deep blue and cloudless as it appears through the canopy.

The walk is brisk and invigorating as we leave the trees and enter the orchard containing its communal crop of kenaf. I also recognize asparagus spears, onion and garlic along with carrot tops. At the far edge of the orchard we encounter fronds of artichoke and brilliant lavender falling away into a treeless valley.

Leeitus gestures me to a halt.

In the distance I am witness to a row of Sasquatch quickly working their way up the valley in our direction. There appears to be about twenty or so of them in single file, loping and chanting a guttural cadence that travels up through the valley. Its sound puts me on edge.

"Loquius is with them," Leeitus tells me, "they will enter Cross Over to the North and meet the stream where I found you yesterday. It is there the ceremony of exile will take place."

The word exile hits me like a slap in the face.

"Loquius is being banished?" I ask, feeling overcome by a terrible sense of guilt and shock.

"Loquius is an elder and a guardian. It is his duty to guard and maintain the boundary between our worlds. You are not supposed to be here, but neither is our kind supposed to cross over to your side. Punishment for multiple illegal crossings is exile," Leeitus explains.

I think of all the Bigfoot sitings across our world. Most, if not all of those reported, are of the aggressive and scary nature, nothing like my friendly encounters with Loquius and his family. Those being exiled to our side must find themselves extremely traumatized— a Sasquatch post traumatic stress, so to speak.

"My father is quite tolerant and reluctant to impose such harsh punishment, but Damarcus is a renegade and a trouble maker to The Council," Leeitus says and speeds us along. I have to jog to keep up.

"Damarcus?" I question and hear the chants of the many big feet falling like rain on the forest.

"We must hurry," Leeitus says and doubles his strides. I am now running to keep pace as Big Creek comes into view. It is the pool at the end of the rapids from which I had emerged into Cross Over where Leeitus plunges into the water. We cross the stream and move up the ridge from the bank to where the trees and brush are thick and untamed.

"If you stand in my shadow they will not know or sense you are here," Leeitus states and shows me where to stand. I can see through the gap between his arm and chest and watch in awe as the Sasquatch procession exits the trees and approaches the creek.

At the head of the procession is Loquius and I sense his eyes penetrate beyond the barrier of Leeitus and lock on my own. I immediately get a vivid picture of the aggressive Sasquatch that had screamed at me and I immediately surmise that his name is Damarcus. He is the one to be banished to our side, a place where he will soon run renegade and apparently fend for himself.

I do not fully comprehend what I am seeing. It is almost as if I have been drugged or hypnotized by the combined forces of so many Sasquatch congregated in front of me. The proceedings that ensue are quite formal and serious with what appear to be multiple opportunities for Damarcus to recant his wrongdoings. Damarcus stands staunch and does not budge, he simply stands erect and shakes his head no to each of the opportunities to confess and get straight.

I feel Leeitus flinch and at the same time feel a change in the surrounding air pressure causing my ears to pop. I must have been lost deep in my thoughts, because when I look up Demarcus is gone, simply banished into exile without so much as a goodbye or word of encouragement.

Silence has descended over the forest. The exile has come to an abrupt end. I watch as Loquius conducts one last ritual and the congregation of Sasquatch are dismissed, turn on their heels and head back the way they had come.

"You must find your own way home," Leeitus tells me. "Remember, listen to the stone and follow the water."

With that he scurries down the ridge, crosses the creek and slips stealthily into the trees.

The experience has left my whole body abuzz. I have to consciously gain control of my runaway heart by kneeling and taking some slow, deep breaths. My head is foggy and my situation seems very unreal. I find myself overcome with being tugged and pulled in two completely different directions, in that I want to go "home", but at the same time I feel strangely compelled to follow Leeitus and Loquius back into the forest of Cross Over.

In the wake of the exile I am standing perplexed as to why I have been left to the mercy of my own devices. Common sense tells me that if I am expected to find the vortex or portal or whatever it is that will deposit me back into my human world, then I could also use it to return to Cross Over anytime I please.

I descend the ridge and wade across the pool to the spot of the exile. I assume the portal has to be very near for Damarcus' abrupt disappearance. Once again, the surrounding forest is alive with wildlife proportioned in size to the Sasquatch. I see a toad the size of my head and envision a bear the size of an elephant. I decide that wondering off on my own may not be a good idea and pull the lapis stone from my pocket to look for any signs of the portal. As I finger the stone and look into its pristine blue, there is no portal to be seen, just a clear vision of the Sasquatch trail leading back into the forest.

Instead of heading south along the creek or southwest in the direction Leeitus has gone, I strike out due west, taking the trail by which the tribe of Sasquatch had paraded in and away from the exile ceremony. Within the energized stone, I am looking at a clear replica of Loquius' face giving me that long penetrating look he had directed towards me just prior to the ceremony. It is beckoning and impelling me to follow.

For whatever reason the whole experience is reminiscent of Alice in Wonderland as I move through the forest and enter the valley where I had first witnessed, along with Leeitus, the chanting parade of Sasquatch. I expect to see a rabbit with a top hat or a hookah smoking caterpillar come dancing down the path to greet me. What I see instead, are huge butterflies with two foot wingspans and honey bees the size of my fist. The cadence of their activity is extraordinary in sound and vibration as they move about in the floral scented air. I detect wild roses, sweet pea blossoms, purple vetch and wafts from clustered pompoms of pink and purple clover.

There isn't any sign of the retreating Sasquatch except for the rutted path on which I continue to make my way. I am now headed south instead of west and I am looking up the rise to where Loquius' orchard and plots of kenaf kiss the oak forest. I wonder if Leeitus is up there somewhere, dutifully watching over my visionary movements away from home and deeper into the strange land of Cross Over.

As I ascend up and out of the valley, I once again enter a forest of sorts, but instead of huge oaks or another of Michigan's native trees, I am among huge bamboos that look to be planted in clumps like a crop of celery. There is plenty of space between the clumps where the kenaf plant I recognize is leafing out thick as the tag alders I am so used to battling on the banks of Big Creek.

I am suddenly jolted alert by the approaching chant of Sasquatch and quickly slip off the path and duck into the heavy cover afforded by the lush kenaf. I barely have time to settle in and hold my breath before the chanting Sasquatch descend on me with great speed. They flash past with remarkable strides and head on up the path into the valley from which I have just come.

I exhale in relief. Now what? I have no plan and the stone in my hand has gone mute. From somewhere out of my youth a song rises up and pulses through my mind. "Should I stay or should I go. If I stay there will be trouble, if I go there will be double."

I am struck by the fact that I am completely unprepared to go on. To do so without food, water and other basic survival needs would be insane. Yet, the stone and the vision…. push, pull.

I know in order to act that I have to be certain of the action to be taken, yet I am now inexplicably frozen by uncertainty and indecision. On the one hand, my knowingness tells me I am acting insane (an indecision resulting in the compulsion to stop what one is doing). On the other hand, I feel experientially compelled to stop what I am doing because the inherent risks dictate reversing the impulsive decision that now has me frozen in a patch of kenaf. I could spend considerable time arguing with myself about this compulsive attempt to escape reality, but it would surely and truly lead me completely out of my gourd. I suddenly understand the significance of what Tecumseh had meant when he told me to be careful of getting caught between my world and that of the Sasquatch. He had shaken his head and warned me that he might not be able to bring me back.

It is beginning to rain, one of the things I am not prepared for. I am dressed in my hiking clothes—long camouflage pants and a matching long sleeved shirt that were meant to protect me from the bugs and sun, but little else. I would go so far as to call myself an idiot fresh off the bus if I were looking at some other person in my position. I just wasn't thinking with all my faculties before I acted. Curiosity, spontaneity, shock; they all got the best of me. It had just never occurred to me that I'd be faced with a prolonged stay in Cross Over.

I figure that I have traveled about a couple of miles from the spot I encountered the chanting Sasquatch on the trail. Since that point, it has been non-eventful except for the the rain that has me drenched. Thankfully it is letting up and the sun is peaking through the hazy fog that is popping up from the humidity. The mosquitos and gnats are also out in force. Cross Over may be an ingenious model for agriculture and environmental science, but it still harbors a multitude of flying pests.

In a spot of sunlight, I take a break and remove my boots to save my feet from blisters. It feels good to be barefoot and let my toes air out and breathe. The sun, for whatever reason has also miraculously dispersed the bugs, allowing me to sit still and gather myself in meditative silence. In with the good, out with the negativities.

Back on the trail, I am once again moving with decision and certainty. I am no longer stuck in a "maybe". I am more relaxed and my spirits are high, but I am now getting hungry. I had been able to quench my thirst in the downpour by cupping my hands and drinking my fill of rain water. It had been sweet and soft, but food was now an issue since I had brought nothing with me. Thankfully, with my wits back in place, I have been noticing the plant kenaf once again growing in bunches beside the trail. Snatching a few leaves, I decide to indulge in a meal of their salty fingers. I do find them quite coarse but eatable, especially the young shoots which are much less prickly in my mouth. I immediately feel more refreshed and poke about, gathering some asparagus spears and wild carrots to round out my meal. It is all quite nourishing and I am energized and ready to make my way deeper into Cross Over.

When confronted with the realm of the unknown, confidence and certainty are definitely the life jackets on which we have to rely. Without them, we are at the mercy of our lesser human emotions and reactions, such as fear, anger, and despair. The vibration of emotion in one person can ignite a like emotion and vibration in another, like a tuning fork. I believe that is the case even with animals. If I fear a dog, that dog is likely to fear me. On the other hand, if I approach a dog with confidence and certainty, that dog is likely to respond in a like manner.

It is not a dog, however, I meet on the trail. It is a wolf the size of a horse that freezes in its tracks and eyes me with gold-flecked orbs whirling with an abyss of black intensity. It raises its nose from the trail and retracts its lips in a grimace that bares long white fangs.

I know that it is no time to panic or react defensively. What happens in the first few nano seconds of an encounter is what can determine the outcome of such a meeting. I know better than to pause or diminish my presence, so I simply continue walking forward towards the wolf as if I own the trail into which he has trespassed.

"What's up, boy?" I say in as bold and friendly tone as I can muster.

I visually watch the vibrations of my words wash over the wolf's fur and dispel the building aggression in its eyes and lips. It is replaced by a quizzical look and a slight bowing of the head.

A shrill whistle disturbs the moment and the wolf gives me one last curious look, then turns and bounds off up the trail. It yips and jumps playfully about as a young Sasquatch unexpectedly appears on the trail. As with the wolf, I have no other option but to walk forward as if I belong there as much as they. I reflexively raise my arm in a gesture of greeting.

The young Sasquatch says something incomprehensible and stops. Seeing me progressing forward, it commands the wolf to its side with a slap of his thigh and another whistle.

I have progressed to within about twenty feet when I pause.

"Loquius," I say, and raise my hand to my brow. I make a gesture as if I am looking for someone and immediately notice understanding registering in the young Sasquatch's eyes. He turns and looks up the trail behind him. He raises his arm and points in the direction I am headed.

I smile and move forward into their immediate space and pass close enough to reach out and scratch the wolf on the chin. Once behind me, I do not look back until I am well up the trail. To my relief, there is no one there. The boy and his wolf have moved on.

The sun has begun to descend the horizon when I find myself above a steep cut overlooking what I assume to be Cross Over's version of either the Au Sable or the Ocqueoc River. The trail descends the cut via several switchbacks and ends on a flat spit of white sand below, where several Sasquatch are jovially engaged in work . They are busy with ropes lashed to a huge raft made of logs. The raft is loaded with wooden crates that are open at the top, and I can see they are filled to the brim with fresh-cut greens, possibly kenaf leaves and other food stores. The raft is moving steadily upstream against a strong current.

This group of Sasquatches, with their fluid and rhythmical motions, remind me of Leeitus and Loquiili dexterously weaving their grow mats. I have come to realize that the Sasquatch are far from lumbering and clumsy, their ability to move swiftly and efficiently in tandem is both graceful and complex. Their spirit appears playful, giving, and socially radiant amongst their own kind.

Unlike crews of men, there appears to be no supervisor or boss overseeing and barking orders. Each Sasquatch appears to be self-motivated. All appear to assume responsibility for himself and each of his fellow team members at the same time. There are no slackers or disgruntled grumblers, thus making what I would call a grueling task look more like a ballet or a symphony instead of drudgery. It is apparent they are happy and enthusiastic in their task! Their rhythmical motions and chanting are filled with a strong positiveness that actually vibrates through the air. I can feel it in my chest and bones. I can't help but feel invigorated and happy along with them.

Thus far, I have been very cautious, I have remained undetected as I've woven my way, now deeply into Cross Over, but I am beginning to question my motives of secrecy as I am uplifted by their spirited interplay. What is my purpose here? What am I trying to achieve? Why should I be concerned with secreting my way around after being invited of sorts by Loquius? I have seen no indication my life is in any serious danger from the Sasquatch. It appears they are more enraptured with purpose and kindness than aggression.

All the while I have been observing, I have been also fingering the lapis stone in my pocket and know it is trying to tell me something important. It has grown warm and agitated in my hand, awakened from its slumber by the same vibrations that are reverberating through my bones.

Holding and looking into the stone reminds me of my modern day I-phone. It is as if I am tuned into YouTube and streaming a video of Loquius delivering an address before the Council of Elders. Not only that, I know for certain he is live-streaming me at the same time. I suddenly realize that what I have in my hand is not a stone at all, it is a time portal in itself. In retrospect, being called the stone without time is a misnomer, it should actually be called the stone of all time, places, forms and events.

I spontaneously decide that it is now or never and launch into a raucous version of Hi-Ho, Hi-Ho in time with the chanting Sasquatch and begin my obtrusive descent down a switchback of uncertainty and unknowns.

To Be Continued in Book 2,
**Conversations With Sasquatch,
Cross Over**

GLOSSARY OF TERMS

abhor*- regard with disgust or hate

abject*- experienced to the maximum degree

accosted*- approach and address boldly or
aggressively

adrenalin*- hormone secretion from the adrenal
glands for extra power and energy in times of fear,
excitement, etc.

Al Kaline*- Detroit Tigers baseball power hitter that
batted fourth in the lineup back in the 1960's and
70's. He had many homers during that era

Anishinaabe*- Native Americans, ancestors of the
Chippewa

attuned*- in harmony or agreement

auras*- the electrical and emotional emanations
surrounding a body

auspicious*- a good omen, successful or
prosperous

barred*- imprisoned behind bars

beefsteaks*- an edible mushroom similar to the
morel but much larger and irregular of shape, reddish
brown in color

befuddled*- confused

Beretta*- a brand of handgun

brethren*- archaic plural of brother

cache*- a hidden collection or store of items of
some type

chiha tanka*- Native American name for Sasquatch
or Big Foot

circumnavigating*- going around

conducive*- useful and fitting

conspiratorially*- a planning and acting together

crepuscule*- the hour of twilight

cut*- baseball bat swing

deftly*- skillfully

delusional*- seeing things that aren't there or real

disheveled*- disarranged and untidy

DNR*- Department of Natural Resources

edible*- fit to be eaten

effused*- poured out or forth

egress*- action of going out or leaving

encroached*- trespass or intrude

epitome*- having the characteristics or quality of the whole.

Ernie Harrell*- Radio announcer for the Detroit Tigers

ewer*- pitcher-like container for holding liquids

fingers*- here means the elongated leaves

flap-trap*- a lot of talk

Giigooh na*- Native American name for big fish

grimace- facial expression of pain of dislike

guttural*- from deep in the body

hackles*- neck hairs

hallucinated- saw things that were not actually there

harboring*- holding in

heft*- to lift

hookah*- many tubed smoking pipe

idiosyncrasies*- any personal peculiarity or mannerism

incoherently*- not understandable, gibberish

inexplicably*- unexplainable, not understood

juking*- dodging and darting

kenaf*- a variety of hibiscus plant valuable for its fibers and thousands of other useful properties

makwa*- Native American name for black bear

mangy*- shabby and filthy

manifesto*- a public declaration of aim or intent

massasauga rattlesnake*- rattlesnake the north present in Michigan

Mida*- Native American name for a medicine man or sorcerer

mirthlessly*- without humor

morel mushrooms*- an edible fungi with a conical head and deeply pitted crevices

narcissism*- an excessive interest in or admiration of self, selfishness

Nawak'osis*- Native American name for marijuana

oblivion*- state of being forgotten

overwhelmed*- crushed, made helpless

ozone*- a blue gas discharged from lightning.

perchance*- by some chance

penchant*- a strong liking or taste for

periphery*- at the edge of one's vision

perusal*- a brief glance over

pippsissewa*- Native American name for wintergreen

psychopath*- antisocial personality prone to criminal and violent behavior

pungently*- sharp smelling

racking it up to*- to decide something

redolent*- sweet-smelling, fragrant

reverberated*- echoed

rife*- widespread, prevalent

ruminating*- chewing on

schizophrenic*- a person with a mental disorder characterized by hallucinations or delusions

stealthily*- secretly

succinctly- clearly and briefly

super-max*- federal prison for the most dangerous of criminals

switchbacks*- winding paths of gradual descent down a steep embankment

telepathically*- from mind to mind without speaking

toss my cookies*- throw-up, puke

traipse*- to walk or wander, trudge

trajectory*- path taken through the forest

trek- a long walk or journey

trepidation*- fear or alarm, dread

tyke*- a small child

unequivocally*- in a way that leaves no doubt

unwieldy*- not easily handled

usurp*- take illegally by force

verdant*- covered with green vegetation

wry*- twisted, distorted

The saga continues in Book II of

Conversations With Sasquatch

Cross Over

1

As I descend the switchback, I cannot help but think of Ted Kaczynski, now a kindred spirit of sorts in a bizarre and opaque way. If that lunatic could survive and win over the Sasquatch in Cross Over, then I shouldn't have a whole hell of a lot to worry about.

Maybe I'm as crazy as he was, belting out "Hi-Ho, Hi-Ho, off to work I go" at the top of my lungs in this foreign reality I know very little about.

Now that I have gotten their attention, I notice that I have caused them to lose control of their raft. It is drifting sideways because someone has dropped their line. One Sasquatch has at least temporarily forgotten his duties in order to gesticulate at the strange singing human descending down upon them.

In the confusion, there is at once a frantic tug of war with the raft and its crew as it tries to spin out of control. Then with all efforts by the Sasquatch refocused on the task, my descent is being ignored. I might just as well be a pesky horsefly buzzing out of reach. I just hope a ticked off bruiser doesn't decide to turn and give me a good swat. I don't think I'd be likely to survive.

As I set foot on the spit of sand, the raft is being stabilized with large wooded stakes already driven to loop the ropes. With some quick overhand knots by the Sasquatch, I am suddenly once again the focus of a dozen shocked faces. For some strange reason I get the sense they are more afraid of me than I am of them.

The force of their powerful presence all turned towards me has halted my forward progress. Time has come to a standstill. Though I am not exactly afraid, I am frozen. How long we have been staring at each other with just a few feet of sand between us, is difficult to discern. Probably only seconds, but it feels like forever. The first thing that comes to mind is the stone without time. Its presence in the palm of my hand registers as my only weapon. In what seems like slow motion, I pull it from my pocket and hold up for the Towering Sasquatch to see.

"Loquius," I say, "Loquius."

And yes, that is the honored password in Cross Over. Their gazes turn to each other as the name registers and subdues a major portion of their fears and confusion. There is a quick paced discussion of sorts before their attention returns to the strange little creature staring up at them.

Once again, I am overwhelmed by their size. I once saw a huge grizzly stand on his hind legs to impress me with his attributes, and as big as that grizzly was,

I do not believe that he'd have the courage necessary to stand up to a Sasquatch. These guys are not just big, they are big foot construction worker enormous.

"Loquius," I repeat, trying to keep any hint of uncertainty from my voice.

Again, there is an animated discussion with hands and arms gesticulating about. There seems to be a faction of discord from two or three of the crew. The look in their eyes and their postures suggest I would be in Bigfoot trouble if not for the vote tally being in my favor.

One of the Sasquatch separates from the group and in three long strides is towering over me. I can smell the damp hair, it's not unlike the smell of a dog after going for a swim, not repulsive, but also not an odor of freshness.

"Oooo-de-de-do?" I am sure he is asking me a question. Such a strange sounding language, kind of like R2-D2 in Star Wars.

I only have one answer. "Loquius?" I ask and just like with the Sasquatch boy, I raise my hand to my brow and pretend to look.

Big Boy turns back to the group and appears to get confirmation from the other's yet bewildered looks. He raises his huge arm and points at the raft, then kneels and looks me in the face. With a finger as big around as my wrist, he draws a squiggly line in the sand. He points once more to the raft and moves his finger up the squiggly line to a point where he jabs his finger in the sand.

"Pariseema," he says. "Loquius Pariseema."

I am caught completely off guard when his big arm reaches out and encircles my waist. I am hefted into the air like a rag doll and carried to raft where I am handed up to another Sasquatch that deposits me on a bed of fresh kenaf.

With a flurry of motion, the crew is back to work and I am on a one way ticket to Pariseema.

2

The river is a source of navigation and activity as we traverse the first few bends. I can see Sasquatch fishing from shore and traveling in our wake on small rafts with oars. I notice the tell-tale mounds of homes appearing along the bank and a few wolves are out pacing and barking at our passing.

The first really strange sight is that of a structure that looks similar to a middle-eastern temple. It is white and domed-shaped with spires. It looks to have borrowed its design from human engineering. Once again I am struck by the largess of the facade built to accommodate the Sasquatch instead of man.

We continue upstream and the temple structure finally fades and disappears as we wend a big bend where the river opens into a medium sized lake. Here, the ropes are coiled and huge oars are mounted as the raft is muscled out into the deep. The water is a staggering blue in contrast to the light blue cloud dappled sky. The air has an invigorating quality that makes me want to explode with energy. I can feel the molecules in my lungs rejoice.

The lake is cradled by hills and dotted with buildings built from the same white material that dominated the temple. They look like homes you would see on the hillsides above Santa Barbara, California. The effuse affluence and importance.

At the end of the lake is a pure white a city. It climbs the hillside from the shore to its pinnacle like a huge overflowing glacier. All the building's walls are white, broken only by shadows. It fills me with a sense of cleanliness that no human city has ever achieved. Maybe it is just the whiteness and the simple barrier of distance, but it emanates a beauty I have never experienced from a feat of creative engineering.

The Sasquatch are once again chanting and their oars are biting the water in perfect harmony. The raft is humming along and speedily parting company with the river's shore. I am enjoying my trip. It is like a fantasy inside a dream in which I am wide awake.

Afterward

Thank you for reading this book. If you have made it this far, then you are a believer and have journeyed along into the parallel universe of Cross Over. You have looked into the stone without time and know the future holds a promise of greater things for mankind.

It is a Sasquatch saying that all barriers and all freedoms are self-created and/or self-imposed.

It is on a generous diet of courage and wisdom that all great civilizations come to be. It is even on greater courage and wisdom that they are maintained and expanded upon through certainty and much vigilance.

We are the true caretakers of own souls and the soul of the world on which we live and depend. Heaven is not a place you go, it is a place you create. The same can be said for Hell.

Best Wishes,
Loquius, Master at Arms for the Council of Elders

Michigan author and artist, Richard Rensberry, lives in Fairview, Michigan with fellow author and illustrator, Mary Rensberry. Together they founded QuickTurtle Books® and **BooksMakeBooms.com**. They are authors, illustrators and publishers of over thirty children's books and custom books for small businesses and worthwhile causes.

More QuickTurtle Books

If I Were A Lighthouse
Keepers of the Light
Big ships
Good Thoughts Gathered Together
Christmas Christmas Everyday
Grandma's Quilt
I Wish I Could
Fairview Berries
Float the River
Butterfly Stomach
The Quest We Share
Maple Tree Elves
A Boy and His Dreams
Sasquatch, A Rhyme for Young Readers
and many more

For copies of any of our books, please email us for more information at:

maryandrichard@quickturtlebooks.com

or visit our shopping cart at:

https://www.booksmakebooms.com